< 1 | *Tree in Cemetery near Springfield, Colorado, 1993*

2 | *Caleb Troyer in Turkey Barn, Holmes County, Ohio, 1997*

Abandoned House West of Limon, Colorado, 1993

To Susan for understanding

I have many to thank, and those thanks must begin with Christopher Brookhouse for his rare, bountiful, and unending generosity. I thank Wendell Berry and Gene Logsdon for the inspiration of their work and for gracing this book with their voices. Nan Black for her elegant design and for the fun of working with her. Howard Sacks for including me in his rural life projects over many years. Lewis Hyde, David Lynn, and Stu Schott for their support. And to so many farm families I do not know personally, as well as those I do: the Browns, the Cassells, the Clutters, the Diltses, the Hathaways, the Hawks, the Laymons, the Norrises, the Pealers, the Shinaberrys, the Sprays, and the Troyers.

I would also like to thank both Kenyon College and the Ohio Arts Council, each for multiple grants to support this work.

And my family, Susan, Erica, and Simon, for appreciating what I do and being who they are, I give thanks.

G.S.

GRACE

Safe Harbor Books
P.O. Box 2568
101 Main Street
New London, New Hampshire 03257

Book design by Nanette Black, N. Black Design
Printed by The Stinehour Press, Lunenburg, Vermont, U.S.A.

Library of Congress Catalogue Card Number: 00-102191
ISBN: 0-9665798-3-6

GRACE

•

Photographs of Rural America
by
Gregory Spaid

•

Essay by
Wendell Berry

•

Introduction by
Gene Logsdon

SAFE HARBOR BOOKS • NEW LONDON, NEW HAMPSHIRE

4 | *Behind Home Plate, Monroe Mills Road, Knox County, Ohio, 1994*

INTRODUCTION

We rural people live in dread of one accusation. Call us hicks, rednecks, clodbusters, or shitkickers and we will grin, spit in your eye, and say we're damn proud of it. Just don't accuse us of "puttin' on airs." "Puttin' on airs" is lower even than running for public office. That being the case with us, for better or for worse, Gregory Spaid's photographs portray rural scenes authentically because there is in them not one iota of puttin' on airs, of pretension, of perfumed toilet tissue, of "country" club puffery.

Not since Andrew Wyeth's paintings have works of art compelled me to stare at them, each in turn, *for so long a time*. This compulsion is especially mysterious because Spaid's pictures appear so unassumingly plain. I can't say I even *like* them, whatever that means. *Hypnotize* would be a better word. I just want to stare at them and maybe, after awhile, cry.

For a person who has known intimately scenes like Spaid portrays in this book, the photographs invoke a great sense of loss. There is one picture, of a dilapidated ball diamond backstop, that particularly affects me. I know one just like it, where this very week, the country kids who make up the ball team that our family took from the backroads of our county to the big cities of Ohio and Indiana and Michigan, will hold a celebration of where it all started. But it will be a sad celebration for me. Only one of those boys stayed home here in our county. The rest, all of them the cream of our rural culture, migrated to the cities to chase the money trail. I keep believing the loss was not inevitable, but the fact is that rural culture slowly dies as our young people drift away. And you can see it dying in almost all of Gregory Spaid's photos in this book—see it dying even in the faces of the hardworking, patient people.

The sadness I feel from the pictures comes mostly from the way they suggest the stubborn rural will to endure in the face of helplessness. Spaid calls it *grace*. Economists I know call it stupidity. I spit in their eyes. It is true that a culture, any culture, can't survive today if not built upon the shifting sands of "the economy." But if we accept the loss of what was once our rural heritage, we don't know what to work towards because the "progress" that overwhelms us is itself constantly overwhelmed by something newer. Biology, the foundation of agriculture, can't survive economic chaos, death-marching to the drums of manipulated money interest. When the madness collapses, it will be the *grace* that Spaid captures in his photographs that will pull us through.

Strangely enough, or perhaps not so strangely, the quicksilver permanence contra dancing with change in these photos reminds me of a day when I was driving in South Dakota many years ago, looking for a rancher. For one thing the landscape was much like that in many Spaid pictures. I stopped at one farmstead to ask directions. Where did so-and-so live? Easy, the woman told me. "Just go down the road you're on till you come to where a bunch of cattle are standing under a tree. Turn right at the next road and the place you're looking for is the first house you come to."

I did not question her directions. This was still a culture that had permanence. If cows would be standing where she said, I wasn't going to doubt her. And sure enough, they were.

Gene Logsdon

5 | *Four Sheep near Amity, Ohio, 1992*

A FEW WORDS FOR MOTHERHOOD

by Wendell Berry

It is the season of motherhood again, and we are preoccupied with the pregnant and the unborn. When birth is imminent, especially with a ewe or a mare, we are at the barn the last thing before we go to bed, at least once in the middle of the night, and well before daylight in the morning. It is a sort of joke here that we have almost never had anything born in the middle of the night. And yet somebody must get up and go out anyway. With motherhood, you don't argue probabilities.

I set the alarm, but always wake up before it goes off. Some part of the mind is given to the barn, these times, and you can't put it to sleep. For a few minutes after I wake up, I lie there wondering where I will get the will and the energy to drag myself out of bed again. Anxiety takes care of that: maybe the ewe has started into labor, and is in trouble. But it isn't just anxiety. It is curiosity too, and the eagerness for new life that goes with motherhood. I want to see what nature and breeding and care and the passage of time have led to. If I open the barn door and hear a little bleat coming out of the darkness, I will be glad to be awake. My liking for that always returns with a force that surprises me.

These are bad times for motherhood—a kind of biological drudgery, some say, using up women who could do better things. Thoreau may have been the first to assert that people should not belong to farm animals, but the idea is now established doctrine with many farmers—and it has received amendments to the effect that people should not belong to children, or to each other. But we all have to belong to something, if only to the idea that we should not belong to anything. We all have to be used up by something. And though I will never be a mother, I am glad to be used up by motherhood and what it leads to, just as—most of the time—I gladly belong to my wife, my children, and several head of cattle, sheep, and horses. What better way to be used up? How else to be a farmer?

There are good arguments against female animals that need help in giving birth; I know what they are, and have gone over them many times. And yet—if the ordeal is not too painful or too long, and if it succeeds—I always wind up a little grateful to the ones that need help. Then I get to take part, get to go through the process another time, and I invariably come away from it feeling instructed and awed and pleased.

My wife and son and I find the heifer in the far corner of the field. In maybe two hours of labor she has managed to give birth to one small foot. We know how it has been with her. Time and again she has lain down and heaved at her burden, and got up and turned and smelled the ground. She is a heifer—how does she know that something is supposed to *be* there?

It takes some doing even for the three of us to get her into the barn. Her orders are to be alone, and she does all in her power to obey. But finally we shut the door behind her and get her into a stall. She isn't wild; once she is confined it isn't even necessary to tie her. I wash in a bucket of icy water and soap my right hand and forearm. She is quiet now. And so are we humans—worried, and excited too, for if there is a chance for failure here, there is also a chance for success.

I loop a bale string onto the calf's exposed foot, knot the string short around a stick which my son then holds. I press my hand gently into the birth canal until I find the second foot and then, a little further on, a nose. I loop a string around the second foot, fasten on another stick for a handhold. And then we pull. The heifer stands and pulls against us for a few seconds, then gives up and goes down. We brace ourselves the best we can into our work, pulling as the heifer pushes. Finally the head comes, and then, more easily, the rest.

We clear the calf's nose, help him to breathe, and then, because the heifer has not yet stood up, we lay him on the bedding in front of her. And what always seems to me the miracle of it begins. She has never calved before. If she ever saw another cow calve, she paid little attention. She has, as we humans say, no education and no experience. And yet she recognizes the calf as her own, and knows what to do for it. Some heifers don't, but most do, as this one does. Even before she gets up, she begins to lick it about the nose and face with loud, vigorous swipes of her tongue. And all the while she utters a kind of moan, meant to comfort, encourage, and reassure—or so I understand it.

How does she know so much? How did all this come about? Instinct. Evolution. I know those words. I understand the logic of the survival of the fittest: good mothering instincts have survived because bad mothers lost their calves: the good traits triumphed, the bad perished. But how come some are fit in the first place? What prepared in the mind of the first cow or ewe or mare—or, for that matter, in the mind of the first human mother—this intricate, careful, passionate welcome to the newborn? I don't know. I don't think anybody does. I distrust any mortal who claims to know. We call these animals dumb brutes, and so far as we can tell they are more or less dumb, and there are certainly times when those of us who live with them will seem to find evidence that they are plenty stupid. And yet, they are indisputably allied with intelligence more articulate and more refined than is to be found in any obstetrics textbook. What is one to make of it? Here is a dumb brute lying in dung and straw, licking her calf, and as always I am feeling honored to be associated with her.

The heifer has stood up now, and the calf is trying to stand, wobbling up onto its hind feet and knees, only to be knocked over by an exuberant caress of its mother's tongue. We have involved ourselves too much in this story by now to leave before the end, but we have our chores to finish too, and so to hasten things I lend a hand.

I help the calf onto his feet and maneuver him over to the heifer's flank. I am not supposed to be there, but her calf is, and so she accepts, or at least permits, my help. In these situations it sometimes seems to me that animals know that help is needed, and that they accept it with some kind of understanding. The thought moves me, but I am never sure, any more than I am sure what the cow means by the low moans she makes as the calf at last begins to nurse. To me, they sound like praise and encouragement—but how would I know?

Always when I hear that little smacking as the calf takes hold of the tit and swallows its first milk, I feel a pressure of laughter under my ribs. I am not sure what that means either. It certainly affirms more than the saved money value of the calf and the continued availability of beef. We all three feel it. We look at each other and grin with relief and satisfaction. Life is on its legs again, and we exult.

Young Draw Horses near Waterford, Ohio, 1994 | 6

7 | *Farm Across Field, Killduff Road, Knox County, Ohio, 1996*

8 | *Pealer's Farm, Summer, Amity, Ohio, 1992*

9 | *Pealer's Farm, Winter, Amity, Ohio, 1993*

Pealer's Barn, Summer, Amity, Ohio, 1992

Partially Painted Barn, Killduff Road, Knox County, Ohio, 1995 | 11

Oshkosh Elevator, Oshkosh, Kansas, 1993 | 12 >

ELEVATOR

<13 | *Restored Prairie Church, Atwood, Kansas, 1996*

14 | *Cross at Chimayo, New Mexico, 1990*

15 | *Christmas Decorations, Martinsburg, Ohio, 1992*

Amish Farm Auction near Nunda, Ohio, 1995 | 16

17 | *Tree on Clutter's Farm, Autumn, Knox County, Ohio, 1996*

18 | *Donald Herrera, Post Maker, near Santa Fe, New Mexico, 1995*

Kelly Baughman Washing Her Horse, Knox County Fair, Mount Vernon, Ohio, 1995 | 19

Marilyn Wood, Motorcycle Rodeo, Chillicothe, Ohio, 1997 | 20>

<21 | *Bonnie Ewing at the Senior Citizen Center, Dalton, Nebraska, 1996*

22 | *Interior of an Abandoned Farm House, Vanatta Road, Knox County, Ohio, 1995*

Ebersole

Piano at Harrison Grange, Knox County, Ohio, 1997

24 | *Capitol Theater, Springfield, Colorado, 1993*

CAPITOL
CAPITOL
COMING SOON
NOW SHOWING
WE HAVE MOVED
SEE YOU AT KARVU
C
JURASSIC PARK

Store Front with Border, Melbeta, Kansas, 1993

26 | *Simple House, Mississippi Delta, Louisiana, 1991*

27 | *Shed, Rich Hill, Ohio, 1995*

Simple Building, Bird City, Kansas, 1993 | 28

Dorema Community Hall, Knox County, Ohio, 1994 | 29>

DOREMA
COMMUNITY HALL

OWL CREEK
HARMONY
PRIMITIVE BAPTIST
CHURCH

< 30 | *Owl Creek Church near Waterford, Ohio, 1994*

31 | *Boarded Church Window, Centerburg, Ohio, 1995*

32 | *Porch of an Abandoned Farm House, Knox County, Ohio, 1995*

LOT FOR SALE
BARN SALE
FRI, SAT SUN
5AC. OR MORE
6324 GRAHAM

Barn Sale Sign, Route 36, Knox County, Ohio, 1993 | 33

Partially Carved Buffalo, Pojoaque Pueblo, New Mexico, 1995 | 34 >

DO NOT
TOUCH

< 35 | *Back of a Biker, Motorcycle Rodeo, Chillicothe, Ohio, 1991*

36 | *Couple Holding Hands, Motorcycle Rodeo, Chillicothe, Ohio, 1996*

PORTA
KLEEN

37 | *Bikers, Motorcycle Rodeo, Chillicothe, Ohio, 1990*

ROYAL ORDER OF THE CRUTCH
LIVE TO RIDE
RIDE TO LIVE

Glenn and Rex Spray on their Organic Farm, Knox County, Ohio, 1995

39 | *Janet Hawk in her Hydroponic Greenhouse, Knox County, Ohio, 1995*

Pumpkins for Sale, Monroe Mills Road, Knox County, Ohio, 1993

SUAIN'S
LEEKS
SHALLOTS
$1.50 LB
SHALLOTS →
9/10 MI. SUAIN'S $1.50 LB

Produce Sign on Route 36 near Centerburg, Ohio, 1993 | 41

Trout Fishing Sign, Zolman Road, Knox County, Ohio, 1995 | 42 >

TROUT
FISHING

10

<43 | *Building #10, Fairgrounds, Bird City, Kansas, 1996*

44 | *Closed Theater, Lakin, Kansas, 1996*

ICE
CREAM
TAMALES

Wall of Country Store, Galisteo, New Mexico, 1992 | 45

Anthony Martinez with his Father's Low Rider, Española, New Mexico, 1995 | 46>

VIGIL STORE
HORNETS

< 47 | *Judge Wendell Cheney at his Retirement Home, McCook, Nebraska, 1993*

48 | *Eric Dilts Collecting Maple Sugar, Knox County, Ohio, 1995*

ALLIS-CHALMERS

49 | *Harvesting Popcorn, Clutter's Farm, Knox County, Ohio, 1996*

Trees Reflecting in Pond, Knox County, Ohio, 1995 | 50

51 | *Stand of Trees near Danville, Ohio, 1990*

Yarman Road near Wooster Road, Knox County, Ohio, 1992

53 | *Section Road Signs, Western Colorado, 1998*

RD 20
RD 47

Grove Church Road with Clouds, Knox County, Ohio, 1990 | 54

Airplane on Fence Post, Simmons Church Road near Mount Liberty, Ohio, 1993 | 55 >

< 56 | *Pegasus Sign, Tribune, Kansas, 1993*

57 | *Jane Laymon's Horse Farm near Gambier, Ohio, 1995*

58 | *Jagers' Farm Sign near Wiley, Colorado, 1996*

JAGERS

Ramada at Monument Valley, The Navajo Reservation, 1991 | 59

Amish Baked Goods Sign, Knox County, Ohio, 1996 | 60 >

BAKED
GOODS
½ Mile
First House on Left

CHESTS

< 61 | *Chests Sign in the Snow, Knox County, Ohio, 1995*

62 | *Farm in Snow off Gilchrist Road, Knox County, Ohio, 1993*

Trees off Nunda Road, Knox County, Ohio, 1995 | 63

Barbed Wire Coil, Gilchrist Road, Knox County, Ohio, 1993 | 64 >

< 65 | *Satellite Dish, Pealer's Farm, Amity, Ohio, 1995*

66 | *Grace Cemetery, McDonald, Kansas, 1996*

GRACE CEMETERY
FOR CEMETERY INFORMATION CALL: W. MARTIN - 2400

PLAIN PICTURES

There is something plain about America that can be experienced most clearly in rural places. It can be heard in unpretentious speech, seen in unadorned buildings, and felt in wide-open spaces. I have photographed this humble quality in various places throughout the United States, but most often on the high plains of Colorado, Kansas, and Nebraska, and in Knox County, Ohio, where I live.

I made the first photographs in this book in 1990, but the actual beginning of the book probably occurred earlier, in 1987, when I returned with my family from living in Italy to see America with fresh eyes. What I saw was that America is still young—after a mere 200 years or so—and that rural America, in many ways, is still the frontier. I saw an aesthetic quite different from what I had seen in Europe: a beauty that was commonplace, austere, utilitarian, hopeful, and yet temporary. Rural America seemed built for the moment, from materials that hardly last a lifetime. Entire towns are disposable and now are slowly melting back to the earth like last year's sunflowers.

There is a palpable melancholy in much of rural America, a sense of premature loss that may explain why so many of these photographs deal with abandonment. But there is also hope, which springs from the resilience of the land and its spiritual power in the lives of people. This is what I mean by "grace" in the title of this book. *Grace* is a word with many shades of meaning, and many of those seem appropriate to rural places: a condition of being favored; a dispensation; a beneficent virtue; mercy; forgiveness; and strength to endure trial. By *grace* I also mean to describe the aesthetic response many people have that binds them to the land despite difficult odds—a condition that contributes to the heartache experienced by many farm families forced to leave farming, as so many have over the course of the twentieth century. Also, I hope the act of making these photographs has its own grace, in the sense of conferring honor or dignity, showing favor and giving pleasure.

It is possible in some parts of western Kansas to pull off to the side of the road—as I have many times to make photographs—turn off the engine and experience an almost perfect silence. No singing birds or clattering tractors, no shouts of children, no trucks whining in the distance. At moments like these the silence seems to congeal around me, more a presence than an absence, solid and full. There are complex reasons for this silence, reasons of history, geography, biology, religion, economics, and weather. Reasons that help to explain, for instance, why the population of many of these counties dropped in the 1990's to levels below that of the 1890's when Frederick Jackson Turner declared the passing of the American frontier. This is not a simple silence.

I have chosen to make these photographs of rural America in a style appropriate to their subject—a plain style. I have tried to present my subjects directly and without artifice or irony. It is the subject that matters to me, not artful strategies of representation. If there is art here, it is the art of clarity and selection. Like the silence, these pictures of plain things are themselves plain . . . but not simple.

Gregory Spaid
Gambier, Ohio
June 2000

Rolling High Plains, Eastern Colorado, 1993 | 67

Krause Road near Centerburg, Ohio, 1995 | 68 >